FREEDOM FLYERS

Text by Jack Harris

A GOLDEN BOOK • NEW YORK

Western Publishing Company, Inc., Racine, Wisconsin 53404

© 1991 Actimagination, Inc. All rights reserved. Printed in the U.S.A. No part of this book may be reproduced or copied in any form without written permission from the publisher. GOLDEN, GOLDEN & DESIGN, GOLDENCRAFT, A GOLDEN BOOK, A GOLDEN LOOK-LOOK BOOK, and A GOLDEN LOOK-LOOK BOOK & DESIGN are trademarks of Western Publishing Company, Inc. Library of Congress Catalog Card Number: 90-81117 ISBN: 0-307-12592-0/ISBN: 0-307-61259-7. (lib. bdg.)

A B C D E F G H I J K L M

Here come the freedom flyers! High in the air, a squadron of sleek jets whizzes by at supersonic speed. Each plane trails a thin line of vapor across the sky. Their roaring engines drown out every other sound. What are these magnificent machines that soar so fast and so high above us?

The Wright Brothers flew the first plane on December 17, 1903. By World War I, planes were being designed for warfare. When World War II began, thousands of bombers were built to fight the world's first war in the air! Today, with modern super-scientific technology, the military protects the skies of the United States by using jets armed with mighty weapons and amazing speed. Together, these planes, their pilots, and ground technicians make up the freedom flyers!

Badge of Honor

Just as professional sports teams have special emblems to identify team members, each squadron has its own special patch. These patches are like badges of honor, proudly worn by pilots and crew members who have studied and worked long hours to earn them.

This is the emblem of the Navy's "Wildcats" VFA-131 Strike Fighter Squadron. The "Wildcats" have seen action in Grenada and Libya, flying in their F/A-18 Hornets.

The VF-111 "Sundowners" Fighter Squadron earned its name by shooting down Japanese planes bearing the "Rising Sun" symbol during World War II. Now its flyers defend freedom around the world in their F-14 Tomcats.

The pilots of VFA-131 Strike Squadron proudly display their "Wildcat" emblem as they gather in front of their F/A-18 Hornets.

F-16 Fighting Falcon

The F-16 weighs seven and a half tons but it's one of the most maneuverable fighter jets ever manufactured. Built in the United States, the Fighting Falcon defends many countries around the world.

When fully armed, an F-16 has a 20mm cannon mounted on its fuselage. Weapons can also be attached to the four pylons under its wings. Air-to-air missiles can be mounted to the F-16's wing tips. All in all, the F-16 is considered the best air-to-ground fighter jet ever assembled!

The 421st Tactical Fighter Squadron, the "Black Widows," flew the first F-16 Fighting Falcons in 1980. This combat-ready squadron has seen action in World War II and flew over 15,400 combat missions in Vietnam.

The Air Force "Thunderbirds" exhibition team flying its F-16 Fighting Falcons.

Flying Fact: The Air Force "Thunderbirds" can fly their F-16's at 450 miles per hour with their wing tips only three feet apart!

Each F-15 costs 30 million dollars!

F-15 Eagle

With a rotary cannon in its fuselage, along with four Sparrow and four Sidewinder air-to-air missiles, the F-15 Eagle is an all-weather, air-superior freedom flyer. The Eagle has a sophisticated radar system secured in its nose cone. This radar system has a range of 200 to 400 miles. Its turbofan engines can propel the F-15 Eagle to a top speed of 1,653 miles per hour!

The "Hat in the Ring" is the emblem of the Air Force's 94th Tactical Fighter Squadron. This legendary squadron spent a total of 2,000 flying hours learning to handle its F-15 Eagles. Its history includes World War II antisubmarine missions and modern-day air defense.

A one-man Eagle aircraft is called an F-15A; a two-man Eagle is designated an F-15B.

F-14 Tomcat

Streaking across the sky at 1,564 miles per hour is the
F-14 Tomcat. The Tomcat's speed comes from two turbofan
engines and "swing" wings. Many pilots and military men
consider the F-14 the ultimate air-combat weapon system.

*The F-14 Tomcats are always based on aircraft carriers at
sea. These amazing machines are armed with Sidewinder
heat-seeking missiles.*

The F-14 Tomcat Doppler Long Range Pulse Radar System can track 20 targets at once and from a distance of 100 miles. The Tomcat can also fire at six targets at the same time.

The "Jolly Rogers" patch is the emblem of the VF-84 Fighter Squadron. The "Jolly Rogers" squadron has a heroic history. In World War II it destroyed 154 enemy aircraft and sank 7 ships. More recently, the "Jolly Rogers" flew their F-14 Tomcats during the Iran Hostage Crisis and the Libyan Gulf incident.

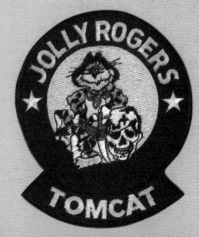

F-14 Tomcat

F-4 Phantom II

F-15 Eagle

F/A-18 Hornet

F-16 Fighting Falcon

Look at these thrilling photographs of the freedom flyers. The next time a jet aircraft screams overhead, see if you can identify the aircraft!

AH-64 Apache

A-10 Warthog

A-10 Warthog

The A-10 Warthog is an airborne fortress. It can carry 12,000 pounds of weapons outside its shell. This includes guided missiles, rockets, and bombs. A General Electric GAU-8 seven-barrel 30mm gun is mounted in its nose, ready to defend against any oncoming enemy.

The pilot is the only one responsible for all 25 tons of this remarkable jet.

The A-10 Warthog's nickname is the A-10 Thunderbolt II.

AH-64 Apache

The AH-64 Apache is a two-seater all-weather attack helicopter. It mounts a 30mm Chain Gun automatic cannon under its fuselage. It can also carry rockets or sixteen laser-guided Hellfire missiles. Its rotary blades measure 48 feet across.

The heroic and legendary "Screaming Eagles" squadron of the 101st Aviation Regiment was the first to receive AH-64 Apache Attack Helicopters. The 101st's battlefield record in Vietnam is unmatched. The squadron received two Presidential Unit Citations for heroism in the face of incredible danger.

Flying Fact: The AH-64 can rise at the rate of 2,500 feet per minute!

Three powerful turbo engines power the AH-64 Apaches.

Flying Fact: The F-4 Phantom II was often used as a high-altitude spying plane.

Fast Fact: At top speed, the F-4 Phantom II can race across the sky at 1,500 miles per hour!

F-4 Phantom II

Since its maiden flight in 1958, the F-4 Phantom II has proven to be one of the most successful freedom flyers in history. Many foreign military forces have bought the Phantom II from the U.S. The Phantom II can carry a variety of weapons, including a laser-guided bomb and Sidewinder missiles.

The "Fighting Eagles" of the 334th Tactical Fighters were the first Air Force F-4 Phantom II squadron. This historic squadron saw World War II and Vietnam action and also served with NATO forces.

F/A-18 Hornet

One of the most advanced fighter jets in existence is the
F/A-18 Hornet. Its radar can track many targets at the same
time. Three computer screens in its cockpit keep the pilot
informed of every operation of the plane. Based on aircraft
carriers, the Hornets take off using the carrier's catapult nets.
When F/A-18 Hornets are launched they can go from 0 to 175
miles per hour in under two seconds. They can also fly as
high as 50,000 feet above the Earth.

*Fast Fact: Flying at top speed, the F/A-18 Hornet can
travel 1,190 miles per hour!*

The Navy's exhibition team, the Blue Angels, flies the F/A-18 Hornets.

In 1982, the heroic "Black Knights" VMFA 314th Fighter Attack Squadron was the first tactical squadron to fly the F/A-18 Hornet fighter jets. The brave "Black Knights" have seen action in World War II and Vietnam.

Ground Crew Signals

Before and after a daring mission, or routine maneuvers, it's up to the Carrier Flight Deck Crew to guide the Flying Fighters through safe takeoffs and landings. How many of these hand signals can you learn?

CUT ENGINES

Hand drawn across neck in "throat cutting" motion.

TURN RIGHT

Pull desired wing around with regular "come ahead" and point at opposite brake.

HOLD

Arm raised with fist clench

COME AHEAD

Hands at eye level execute beckoning motions. Rate of motion indicates desired speed of aircraft. For night operation, wave wands side to side.

STOP/APPLY BRAKES

Arms raised up, palms outward, rapidly clench fists.

TURN LEFT

Pull desired wing around with regular "come ahead" and point at opposite brake.

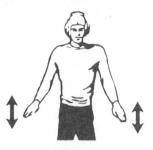

SLOW DOWN

Downward patting motion, hands out at waist level.

TURNOVER OF COMMAND

Both hands pointed at next succeeding taxi signal man.

EMERGENCY STOP

Arms crossed above head, fists clenched.

EMERGENCY SHUTDOWN

Emergency stop signals followed by cut engines.

NIGHT SIGNAL

Same as day signals, except flashlights or wands will substitute for hand and finger movements.

CARRIER FLIGHT DECK PERSONNEL COLOR CODING

RED SHIRTS—

Ordnance and Crash Crew

YELLOW SHIRTS—

PRI Fly, Plane Directors, Catapult Officers, and Arrestment Officers.

BLUE SHIRTS—

Plane Handlers (Pushers, Chock Men, etc.)

PURPLE SHIRTS—

Fuel Handling

GREEN SHIRTS—

Aircraft Maintenance, Catapult Crew, and Arrestment Crew

BROWN SHIRTS—

Plane Captains

WHITE SHIRTS—

Medical Officers
Safety Officers

FREEDOM FLYERS

What will the future bring? Will new technology end the need for fighter jets and fighter pilots? Will computers alone fly the planes of tomorrow? No matter what happens, people will still be needed to design, build, and operate aircraft in the years to come. Who knows, maybe one day *you* will be one of the...FREEDOM FLYERS!